The Little Engine that Could

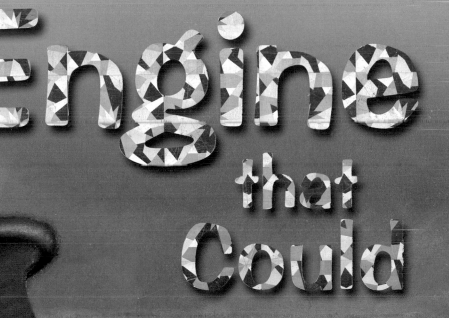

Illustrated by Wendy Straw

There was a little railroad train with loads and loads of toys,

That started out to find a home with little girls and boys,

And as that little railroad train began to move along,

The little engine up in front was heard to sing this song:

    'Choo choo choo choo,

    Choo choo choo choo,

    I feel so good today —

    Oh, hear the track, Oh, clickety clack,

    I'll go my merry way.'

The little train went rousing on so fast it seemed to fly,
Until it reached a mountain that went almost to the sky,
The little engine moaned and groaned,
and huffed and puffed away,
But halfway to the top it just gave up and seemed to say:

'I can't go on,
I can't go on,
I'm weary as can be —
I can't go on,
I can't go on,
This job is not for me.'

The toys got out to push but all in vain alas, alack,
And then a great big engine came a-whistling down the track,
They asked if it would kindly pull them up the mountainside,
But with a high and mighty sneer it scornfully replied:

'Don't bother me, don't bother me,
To pull the likes of you,
Don't bother me, don't bother me,
I've better things to do!'

The toys all started cryin' 'cause that engine was so mean,

And then there came another one, the smallest ever seen,

And though it seemed that she could hardly pull herself along,

She hitched on to the front

and as she pulled she sang this song:

'I think I can,
I think I can,
I think I have a plan —
And I can do most anything
    If I only think I can.'

And up that great, big mountain with the cars all full of toys,

And soon they reached the waiting arms of little girls and boys,

And though that ends the story it will do you lots of good,

To take a lesson from the little engine that could:

Just think you can,

Just think you can,

And have that understood —

And very soon you'll start to say

I always knew I could . . .

I knew I could, I think I can,

I knew I could, I think I can . . .

The Little Engine that Could

The Little Engine that Could is a modern classic and one of the best-loved and well-known of children's songs. Here, artist Wendy Straw brings it to life with her vibrant and animated illustrations.

KO-385-783

A BROLLY Book
ISBN 1-921346-66-3
ISBN 978-1-921346-66-8

9 781921 346668

Children's